HECTOR
THE DESTRUCTOR
LEARNS TO SKATE

WRITTEN BY KIM FEDYK

Hector loved making messes.

He couldn't help it.

No matter what he did, or how hard he tried, he always ended up making a

BIG MESS.

His mom,
his dad,
his grandma,
his grandpa,
his aunts and uncles,
and his kindergarten teacher,

all called him Hector the Destructor.

Today Hector's mom was taking him skating.

He was a little bit nervous. He had never been skating before. But he was also very excited.

"Ready?" His mom asked

"Ready!" Hector said.

When they reached the edge of the rink, Hector's mom stopped him. "Now Hector," she said. "Remember to be careful. The ice is VERY slippery."

"Right. Right," Hector said. "Careful. I got it."

Hector's mom held his hand and helped him step out on to the ice.

He stood for a moment. He didn't fall.

"Pfft," he said. "This is EASY!"

He took a giant lunge forward and lost his balance. He fell hard on his bottom.

"OOOPH," he cried.

He pulled his mom down with him and she fell hard on her stomach.

"ERRPH," she yelled.

Hector slowly picked himself back up. "Sorry mom," he said.

"That's okay," said his mom. "Everyone falls. But let's take it slow okay?"

"Okay," Hector agreed.

He took his mom's hand and together they skated

VERY
        SLOWLY

around the rink.

SO slowly, that Hector was sure it would be summer before they made it around once.

"Mom. This is BORING," Hector complained. "I want to go faster."

"But you are just learning," his mom explained. "You need to start slow."

"Hmph!" Said Hector. "Not fair."

He tore his hand away from his mom's and took two fast glides on his own.

It was AMAZING!
"Hector! Watch out!" His mom yelled. "You are going too fast!"

"I am NOT going too fast!" He yelled back at her.

But he was. He lost his balance and landed heavily on his bottom.

But since he was going so fast, he continued to slide along the ice.

He was headed right for a large group of people.

"Watch out!" Hector yelled at them.

But it was too late.

He crashed into them.

Arms went flying,
legs went flying,
hats and scarves and gloves went flying.

People fell down all around Hector and he disappeared in the pile.

Hector's mom raced over and fished him out.

"Did you see mom?" Hector said excitedly. "I was going so fast!"

"Yes I saw," his mom said.

She looked at the people sprawled in a huge heap on the ice.

Some were trying to stand up,
some were trying to find their lost clothes,
and some were rubbing bruised arms and sore bottoms.

But ALL looked VERY ANGRY.

"Uh maybe we should stop skating for today," she said.

"Okay," Hector said. He was disappointed.

While his mom was pulling him off the ice, Hector spotted a hot chocolate stand by the side of the rink.

"MOM!" Hector said, his disappointment forgotten. "Can I get hot chocolate?"

Hector's mom sighed. "I suppose."

"YAY!" Hector yelled.

He jumped up and down in excitement.

"Hector!" his mom yelled. "Ice is slippery!"

But it was too late.

Hector lost his balance again. He fell onto the ice and rolled out of the rink.

Right into the group of people trying to get on the ice.

Arms went flying,
legs went flying,
hats and scarves and gloves went flying.

People fell down all around Hector and he disappeared under the pile.

Hector's mom fished him out of the mound of people.

She looked at everyone sprawled in a giant heap on the ground.

Some were trying to stand up,
some were trying to find their lost clothes,
and some were rubbing scraped arms and hurt backs.

But ALL looked VERY ANGRY.

"Can we get hot chocolate now?" Hector asked.

"Yes right now!" His mom agreed and pulled him quickly away.

At the hot chocolate stand, Hector ordered the deluxe hot chocolate with extra whipped cream.

"It's going to be hot," his mom warned. "Don't drink it right away!"

"But mom, it's called HOT chocolate for a reason. It's SUPPOSED to be hot."

Hector took a giant gulp.

"HOT!" He yelled, throwing his cup in the air.

HOT !

HOT !

HOT !

He ran around in a circle, waving his arms and screaming.

He wasn't paying attention to where he was going and he crashed right into the hot chocolate stand.

Cups went flying.
Toppings went flying.

The thermos of hot chocolate tipped over and poured out onto the ground.

Hector's mom looked at the mess and frowned.

"Hector! What am I going to do with you?"

She grabbed his hand and pulled him away.

"Let's just sit on this bench for a while and try not to cause any more damage okay?"

Hector sat down on the bench, a big smile on his face.

"Mom I love skating! I want to come back tomorrow."

"What?!!" Said his mom

Hector looked around at the angry people on the ice, the angry people still trying to get on the ice and the puddle of hot chocolate on the ground.

"But maybe we should go to a different rink."

Want more Hector adventures?

Find more titles at www.kimfedykwrites.com

Made in the USA
Monee, IL
15 November 2022

17789322R00019